The Trial of CARDIGAN JONES

by Tim Egan

Houghton Mifflin Company
Boston 2004

To my wonderful cousin, Beth

The text of this book is set in Dante Medium.
The illustrations are ink and watercolor on paper.

Library of Congress Cataloging-in-Publication Data
Egan, Tim.
The trial of Cardigan Jones / by Tim Egan.
p. cm.
Summary: Cardigan the moose goes to trial for stealing an apple pie he swears he only sniffed.
ISBN 0-618-40237-3
[1. Pies—Fiction. 2. Trials—Fiction. 3. Moose—Fiction.] I. Title.
PZ7.E2815Tr 2004   [E]—dc22   2003019400

Printed in Singapore
TWP 10 9 8 7 6 5 4 3 2 1

Cardigan walked by Mrs. Brown's house just as she was putting a fresh-baked apple pie in her window. Cardigan loved pies.

He walked over and smelled the pie. A neighbor next door saw him, and a milkman, driving by, saw him, too. Cardigan was new in town, and they weren't sure what he was up to.

A moment later, Mrs. Brown came back to the window and the pie was gone. She was so upset, she called the police.

She told them that she'd seen a moose just a few minutes before,
so they drove around the block and stopped Cardigan.

Noticing that he had pie crust on his shirt, they arrested him,
even though he insisted he hadn't stolen the pie.

A judge and a jury were chosen to decide if he stole the pie or not.

The neighbor and the milkman were called as witnesses.

Cardigan's trial started the next day. Mrs. Brown took the stand first.

"Is there anyone in this courtroom that you saw the day the pie disappeared?" the judge asked her.

"Yes," she said, "that moose over there." She pointed to Cardigan. There was a murmur from the crowd. "He did it. He's guilty," someone said.

"We don't know that yet," said the judge. The rabbit then took the stand.
"Did you see anyone near the pie?" the judge asked the rabbit.

"Sure did," said the rabbit. "That moose right there. He stole it."

"No, I didn't!" shouted Cardigan. "I didn't steal it! I promise!"

"Order!" shouted the judge. Cardigan turned and his antlers bumped a statue and sent it crashing to the floor.

It made a really loud noise, and the jury gave Cardigan dirty looks.
"Next witness!" shouted the judge.

The milkman then took the stand.

"Who did you see at the time the pie was taken?" the judge asked.

"The moose," he said, "no question about it. He walked right
up to the window. His face was practically touching the pie."

By now, some folks were convinced that Cardigan took the pie, even though the judge kept saying, "We still don't have any proof."

Finally, Cardigan was called to the stand. As he crossed the courtroom, his antlers got all wrapped up in the flag. It took him over a minute to get untangled.

"He's a troublemaker," declared a gopher.

Others nodded in agreement as the judge asked, "Well, moose. Did you walk up to the pie?"

"Well, uh, yes, but just to smell it . . ." said Cardigan softly.

"I knew it!" shouted a goat. "Lock him up!"

"Order!" commanded the judge. "Order in the court!"

"But I didn't take it!" insisted Cardigan. "Honest!"
He stood up, and his antlers knocked the judge's gavel to the floor.

"Sit down!" shouted the judge. But as Cardigan went to sit, he bumped the judge with his antlers.

The judge fell to the ground.

"He hit the judge!" shouted one of the security guards. They grabbed Cardigan and started taking him away. The jury members had made up their minds.

But the judge stood up and said, "Now just hold on a minute!"

"I'm curious about something," he said. "Follow me." He walked out
of the courtroom, and everyone followed him through the town.

They reached Mrs. Brown's house, and the judge walked around
the outside to the window where the pie had been.

Sure enough, there, smushed all over the bushes, was the apple pie.
It didn't smell very good anymore.

"You knocked it off the window with those giant antlers of yours, you silly moose," said the judge, laughing. "It was an accident."

Everyone immediately felt terrible for being so rotten to Cardigan,
and the jury proclaimed him "not guilty" right then and there.

To make it up to him, they had a party in his honor, and Mrs. Brown baked a pie especially for him, even after he broke her favorite vase.